Note to Adults

No Way, Slippery Slick! is designed to be read aloud so that you can engage young children in the storytelling process while introducing them to a very serious topic.

When Slippery Slick tries to tempt Clever Kitten with his colored pills or cigarettes, pause before turning the page and finding out how Clever responds. Invite your child to make up his or her own response. As children become more familiar with the various encounters between Slippery Slick and Clever Kitten, encourage them to create their own stories and solutions.

Reading about Slippery Slick and Clever Kitten is a safe and easy way to initiate discussions about making healthy choices. When we listen to children and give them a chance to practice decision making with us, we empower them to become active participants in the fight against substance abuse.

—Eileen Wasow

Director, Project Healthy Choices

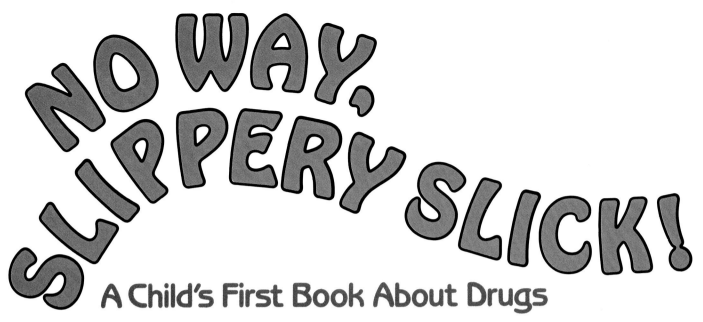

NO WAY, SLIPPERY SLICK!

A Child's First Book About Drugs

Created by Bank Street College of Education

Authors: JOANNE OPPENHEIM   BARBARA BRENNER   WILLIAM H. HOOKS

Illustrator: JOAN AUCLAIR

HarperCollins*Publishers*

Acknowledgments

Project Healthy Choices wishes to acknowledge the special assistance of Queens Borough President Claire Shulman. We are grateful to the New York City Board of Education, whose initial funding supported the development of this book—our thanks to Gwendolyn C. Baker, President of the New York City Board of Education, and her staff: Carol A. Gresser, Irene H. Impellizzeri, Westina L. Matthews, Michael J. Petrides, Luis O. Reyes, Ninfa Segarra, John R. Nolan, Mary C. Tucker, and Wendy Weinstein. We also wish to express our appreciation to Joseph Shenker, President of Bank Street College and to those teachers, counselors, and administrators who participated in the pilot project and helped to revise the curriculum in their schools.

Library of Congress Cataloging-in-Publication Data
Oppenheim, Joanne.
   No way, Slippery Slick! : a child's first book about drugs /
Joanne Oppenheim, Barbara Brenner, William H. Hooks ; illustrator,
Joan Auclair.
       p.   cm.
   "Created by Bank Street College of Education."
   Summary: Clever Kitten refuses to be tempted by drugs and alcohol.
   ISBN 0-06-107438-1 (pbk.)
   [1. Drug abuse—Fiction.   2. Drugs—Fiction.   3. Cats—Fiction.]
I. Brenner, Barbara.   II. Hooks, William H.   III. Auclair, Joan,
ill.   IV. Bank Street College of Education.   V. Title.
PZ7.0616No   1991   90-45163
[E]—dc20   CIP
                                                          AC

NO WAY, SLIPPERY SLICK!

This is the story of Slippery Slick and…

Slippery is one rotten cat…

Clever Kitten.

but Clever is one smart kitten.

Clever Kitten is sitting
on the swing, all alone
with nothing to do.
"It's so boring," says Clever.
"I wish I had something
exciting to do."

FLASH! Here comes Slippery Slick on his flying motorcycle.

"Climb on!" he says.
"We'll fly to places you've never seen.
Don't worry—no one will ever know.
It'll be our secret!"
What does Clever tell that dude
Slippery Slick?

"I only fly on airplanes.
I don't take off with strangers.
I don't take off without
my mom's permission!"

Clever Kitten is getting
cleaned up.
Clever sings,
"This is the way
we wash our paws,
wash our paws,
wash our paws."

Suddenly the medicine cabinet says,
"I've got all kinds of
goodies in here— lots of pills
to make you feel happy.
Just whisper, 'Open Sesame!'
and I'll let you taste my treats!"

What does Clever Kitten
tell that medicine cabinet?

"Keep your goodies to yourself,
medicine cabinet!
I don't need pills
to make me happy.
I never take medicine
by myself."

A mysterious lamp falls from the sky.
It lands at Clever Kitten's feet.
Clever picks it up and rubs it.

Instantly, a genie appears and says,
"I will make you rich
beyond your wildest dreams.
Just take this package to the guys
across that bridge."
Clever Kitten asks
what's in the package,
but the genie won't tell.

What does Clever tell that genie?

Clever Kitten is rushing to the palace
when he meets a fire-breathing dragon.
Smoke is billowing out of his mouth and nose,
and he is coughing.

"Are you all right?"
asks Clever Kitten.
"Just a bit of a cough,"
says the dragon.
"Nice of you to ask.
Would you like to join me
for a smoke?"

What does Clever Kitten
tell that dragon?

Clever Kitten is building a magnificent sand castle.
Suddenly, a knight in shining armor rides in
on the tide.

"Behold!" says the knight.
"Here is a glittering spike of steel.
What a noble flagpole
it would make for your
castle tower.
Why not try it on for size?"

What does Clever Kitten
tell that knight?

"That's no flagpole, knight.

That's a needle.

It's garbage.

I don't play with garbage!"

Clever Kitten and his friends are having a picnic.

"We forgot the lemonade!" cries Clever.

FLASH! A pirate appears.

"Here is something better than lemonade," he says.

"Try this wine cooler.

It'll make you feel real grown-up.

"I dare you to take a swig!" says the pirate.

Everyone except Clever Kitten takes a swig.

"Come on, Clever," they say.

"We dare you!"

What does Clever tell the kids and that pirate?